MONKEY BUSINESS

In loving memory of our Dads
and all we learnt from them

– S.P-H. and D.W.

ORCHARD BOOKS
338 Euston Road, London NW1 3BH
Orchard Books Australia
Level 17/207 Kent Street, Sydney, NSW 2000
First published in 2013 by Orchard Books

Text © Smriti Prasadam-Halls 2013
Illustrations © David Wojtowycz 2013

The rights of Smriti Prasadam-Halls to be identified as the author and of David Wojtowycz
to be identified as the illustrator of this work have been asserted by them
in accordance with the Copyright, Designs and Patents Act, 1988.

A CIP catalogue record for this book is available from the British Library.

ISBN 978 1 40831 378 7

1 3 5 7 9 10 8 6 4 2

Printed in China

Orchard Books is a division of Hachette Children's Books,
an Hachette UK company.
www.hachette.co.uk

MONKEY BUSINESS

Smriti
Prasadam-Halls

ORCHARD

David
Wojtowycz

All was quiet on Noah's big ark.

The sun had set and the sky had grown dark.

When a cry ripped the air,

"Good heavens!" cried Noah.

"Whatever's the matter?

You woke the whole ark with your yells,

Charlie Chatter!"

"I can't find my potty!

I've searched high and low.

Oh, Noah, I'm desperate.

I really MUST go!"

"Charlie Chatter, now, now,
you must surely admit,
Your little old potty is
quite a **tight fit**!

You're getting grown up –
you should try something new.
Say goodbye to your potty . . .
and sit on the loo!"

The monkey wailed, "No!
I can't sit on the loo.
Not for a wee and not for a . . .
p . . . number two!"

"ARK ALERT!" called Noah. "Who has an idea,
Of how to get rid of this **big toilet** fear?"

The snakes hissed,
"There's no finer place for a sssssstory,
Than seated upon the lava-tory.

Step in and see ours,

have a really good look.

It's the perfect place to curl up with a book!"

"Tra-la!" trilled the songbirds.

"From our point of view,

There's no better spot to sing than the loo.

To sing in the rain is a glorious feeling,

But to sing on the loo is much more appealing!"

"For us," mooed the cows,
"when we eat something yummy,
We must wait till it's passed
all the way through our tummy,

Which has **four** different bits,
imagine that!
So we sit on the looooo
for a really long chat."

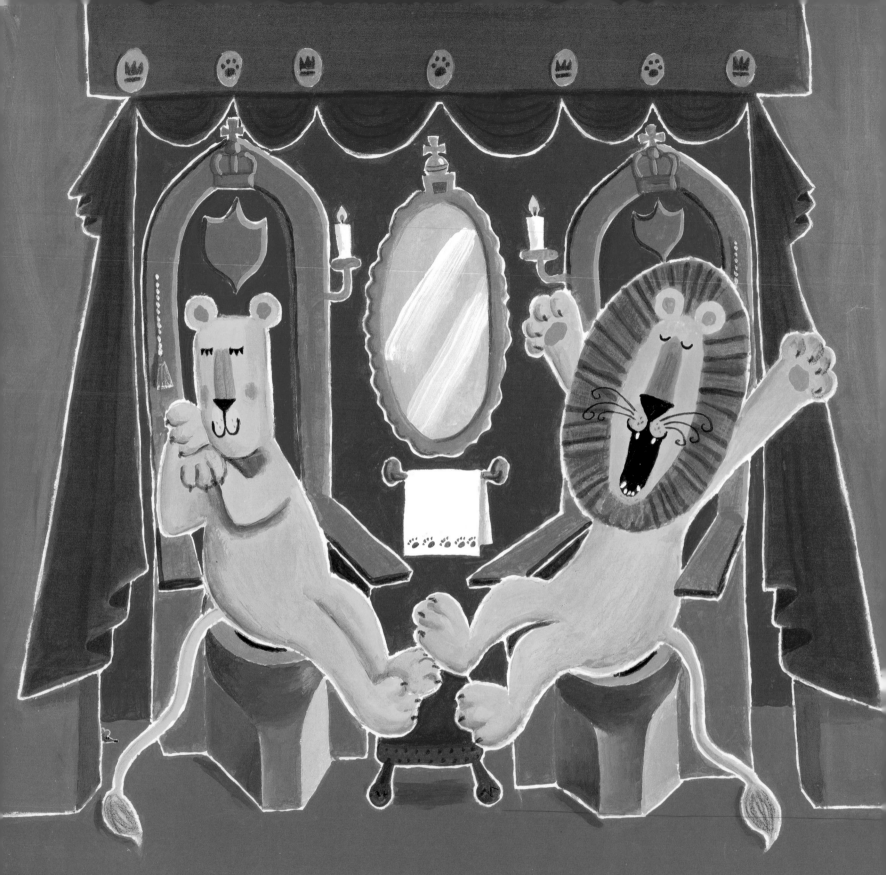

The sleepy old lions yawned, "We love our loos.

It's where we stretch out for a lovely long snooze."

"Oh, no!" snapped the crocs.

"The loo's the best place,

To practise having a brush-your-teeth race!"

Creatures came forward with lots of advice,

Saying, "Time on the toilet is really quite nice!"

Till Charlie agreed, looking less worried,

And off to his very own bathroom he hurried.

But, alas! When he tried the door . . .

. . . it was stuck!

"Oh dear!" said Noah.

"Now that is bad luck!"

The animals pushed with all of their might,

But the door was stuck – and it was stuck tight!

Charlie Chatter cried,

"Let me in – I don't care how –

I have to go . . .

and I have to go

NOW!"

Just then there was heard a "tum-te-te-tum",
A "twiddle-de-dee" and a "rum-pum-pum-pum".

"Mrs Noah?" cried Noah. "Is that YOU in there?"

"Why yes, my dear, I've been making repairs."

"Can you see in the roof there was a big hole?
Well, to catch all the drips I've been using this bowl!

It is small, round and deep and it just did the trick.

I was able to mend the roof ever so quick!"

"My POTTY! It's here!
Why, hello and . . . GOODBYE!
I'm off to give the toilet a try.

If you'll excuse me, I simply can't wait.

I must go right now . . .

or it might be too late!"

"Cheerio . . ." called the monkey
as he skipped to the loo . . .